# RETURN TO THE SEA

By Heidi Jardine Stoddart

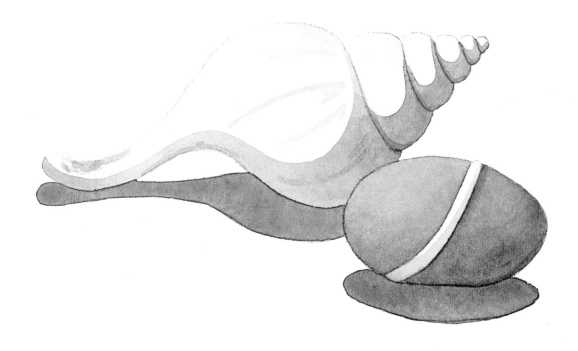

Nimbus Publishing Limited
PO Box 9166
Halifax, NS  B3K 5M8
(902) 455-4286

Printed and bound in Singapore

Design:  Lise Hansen

Library and Archives Canada Cataloguing in Publication

Stoddart, Heidi Jardine, 1967-
  Return to the sea / Heidi Jardine Stoddart.

ISBN 10: 1-55109-606-4     ISBN 13: 978-1-55109-606-3

1. Maritime Provinces—Description and travel—Juvenile fiction.
2. Québec (Province)—Description and travel—Juvenile fiction.
I. Title.

PS8637.T64R48 2007     jC813'.6     C2007-900097-5

We acknowledge the financial support of the Government of Canada through the Book Publishing Industry Development Program (BPIDP) and the Canada Council, and of the Province of Nova Scotia through the Department of Tourism, Culture and Heritage for our publishing activities.

*In memory of my grandparents, Gordon & Dorothy Jones,*
*who first welcomed us to "The Cottage";*
*To Mom, Dad, Tracy & Sherri for all the good times there;*
*To Dwayne, for joining in the fun and always believing;*
*And to everyone who cherishes a special place by the sea.*

# RETURN TO THE SEA

By Heidi Jardine Stoddart

I ❤ NB

FRIENDS 4EVER

Your dearest wish will come true.

## Stuff to Pack ☺

- autograph book
- sweatshirts
- shorts
- bathing suit
- hat
- sunscreen
- sleeping bag
- pajamas
- jeans

When I was quite young, about nine, perhaps ten,
My family travelled down east once again.
When school was let out we'd return to the sea.
"Just one more sleep!" said my sister to me.

We'd head to the cottage just like years before,
But this time we wanted to see even more.
The trailer behind us, we drove the first day,
Then stopped to explore "Vieux Québec" on our way.

A shimmering, sparkling, magical sight
As we ferried across the St. Lawrence that night…
A castle, so welcoming, set all aglow
With an old-fashioned kingdom spread out below.

Next morning, as it was our favourite trip song,
We sang "On the Road Again," driving along.
Our first stop was Hartland for breakfast and tea
Then a walk through the bridge for my sisters and me.

The cottage was next!  Not much further and then…
"There's Nanny and Grampie! We're here!" once again.
The beach!  Oh, I just couldn't wait to get there
And savour that first East Coast breath of salt air.

We searched to find wishing rocks, seashells and snails,
Played pirates and sea monster, mermaids and whales…
Then walked out on barnacled rocks, just to meet
The highest of all the world's tides at our feet.

At full moon the tide was especially high.
We fished for small smelt and we watched seagulls fly.

At low tide the boats gently sank to the sand;
Who'd ever believe boats could stand on dry land?

My Grampie's new tale
was about Captain Lowe
Who sailed his grand ship
to Isle Haute long ago.
"He buried his gold there,
way out in the bay.
Guarded by ghosts,
it's still there to this day!"

While I thought of pirates
and treasures and pearls
My parents announced,
"It's time for bed, girls!
Tomorrow we're off,
with more places to see."
"Come back when you're done,"
Grampie whispered to me.

A cove named for Peggy—we roamed and explored
The rock-riddled place while the sea crashed and roared.
Tried chasing, embracing the wild wind that blew;
Mailed cards from the lighthouse—It's a post office, too!

Nearby, in a rocky cove cradled, we found
The best place to stay! It's a seaside campground!
By day we would play right beside the blue sea…
Go jigging for crabs, which we'd always set free.

At nighttime, a bonfire set all aglow…
As stars in the sky were reflected below
In water so still, we saw stars in the sea.
"It's twice as much heaven," I sighed dreamily.

Next morning, a city of sea tales and charm,
Surrounded by water from Basin to Arm.
We danced 'round a bandstand,

explored an old fort,

Watched tugs welcome ships to the Halifax port.

Next day, the Northumberland
Strait we did sail.
"Watch out for the jellyfish…
maybe a whale!"

The Island was perfect, a storybook land—
Small harbours, quaint farmhouses, red roads and sand!

Of course we saw Anne, and we all longed to be
Just like her, so "New hats with braids!" for all three.

We happily wandered, had ice cream, then found
A touch tank with saltwater life swimming 'round!

We set up our camp along Cavendish Shore,
Where night's lullaby was the waves' distant roar,
After beautiful bike rides along the blue sea,
We left PEI and went back to NB.

The cottage once more, Grampie waiting for me
To share the last days of our trip by the sea.
I had so much to show him and so much to say
About my adventures while I was away.

At last my mom said to give Grampie a rest.
I hugged him and whispered, "The cottage is best!"
I'd waited so long for vacation and then
It went by too fast, time for home once again.

"Farewell little cottage and people so dear...
Stay close in our hearts till we come back next year."